WHO'S CRAZY NOW?

A Comedy in Three Acts

by Gerald Bell

A SAMUEL FRENCH ACTING EDITION

SAMUEL FRENCH

FOUNDED 1830

New York Hollywood London Toronto

SAMUELFRENCH.COM

IMPORTANT BILLING AND CREDIT REQUIREMENTS

All producers of WHO'S CRAZY NOW? *must* give credit to the Author of the Play in all programs distributed in connection with performances of the Play and in all instances in which the title of the Play appears for purposes of advertising, publicizing or otherwise exploiting the Play and/or a production. The name of the Author *must* also appear on a separate line, on which no other name appears, immediately following the title, and *must* appear in size of type not less than fifty percent the size of the title type.

CAST

Nurse Smith
Nurse Jones
The Art Teacher
The Music Teacher
The History Teacher
The Principal
The English Teacher
The Gym Teacher
The Doctor, Mr. Van
The Superintendent, Mr. Arthur
The Superintendent's Niece, Miss Ware
The Insane Doctor, Mr. J. Manchester-Sullivan

First Act: *Noon.*

Second Act: *Evening.*

Third Act: *The following morning.*

Note: *The comedy of this play can be enhanced by substituting the actual names of the people doing the play, particularly if it is produced by school-teachers. For that reason names are not given, but merely the* Art, Music, Gym, *or* History Teacher. *Some lines can be changed to bring in local inferences. This was done by the group who first produced the play, to great advantage.*

DESCRIPTION OF CHARACTERS

NURSE SMITH: *A kindly, good-natured person, preferably rather young.*

NURSE JONES: *An impatient, demanding sort of person, who will never quite get used to the actions of the patients. Probably older than MISS SMITH.*

ART TEACHER: *A tall, dark woman, preferably, who takes her work seriously. She is in a perpetual feud with the MUSIC TEACHER.*

MUSIC TEACHER: *A large, heavy-chested woman, with great and powerful lungs, and does she use them!*

HISTORY TEACHER: *A dramatic, nervous, erratic woman.*

PRINCIPAL: *Serious, never forgetting that she is the PRINCIPAL. A large woman is preferable. She is pompous and bigotted.*

ENGLISH TEACHER: *A joyful person during playtime but serious when she is teaching. She is the chief comedy part and should play it with abandon.*

GYM TEACHER: *Preferably a large woman, very dynamic and with an abundance of energy. She seems to fairly force her way through life. She must also be coy and bashful during her scenes with DR. SULLIVAN.*

DOCTOR VAN: *The leading man type: nice-looking, kind, and jovial.*

MR. ARTHUR: *A man about forty-five or fifty; rather dignified, and inclined to be an "I-told-you-so" type, but still likable.*

FLORENCE WARE: *A petite and chic young woman —not dumb but never quite knowing just what everything is all about in this asylum.*

DOCTOR SULLIVAN: *A very dandified and pompous man of forty-five or fifty. During his scenes he always maintains an air of dignity, until he finally gets the opportunity of trying his theories. In this scene he is almost carried away with his own importance and with joy at his prospects. He should wear a wing-collar and long black tie.*

NOTE: *Ordinary clothing is worn by ALL OTHERS. DR. VAN wears a doctor's apron in the First Scene, and DR. SULLIVAN wears one when he comes from the scene of the operation. FLORENCE WARE should have a hat, coat, and luggage when she enters. Other times just regular clothes.*

PROLOGUE

Note: *The house is completely darkened. The reader of the Prologue comes in front of the curtain, with only a flashlight on his face.*

"There are some things
That I shall say,
So you may know
About this play.

An insane asylum
For crazy teachers
Is the play you'll see
From them thar bleachers.

They go crazy,
As a rule,
Teaching children
Of this school.

Behind their desks,
These women stand—
These noble women,
Best in the land.

But teaching is
The worst of arts.
Especially teaching
These upstarts.

'We lose our heads,
Go quite insane.'
That's a teacher's
Sad refrain.

So we see these teachers
Ten years hence.
The play begins—
Ready? Ladies and Gents!"

*(The CURTAIN has already been drawn up, so
when the Prologue is finished the LIGHTS go
up, and the play begins immediately.)*

Who's Crazy Now?

ACT ONE

Scene: *The reception room of the Sunnyvale Insane Asylum.*

At the Center back is the desk, occupied by the nurse on duty. To the Left of this desk is a window with a green blind that pulls down in front of the curtain, or drapes. To the Left of this is a small table, in front of which is a large comfortable chair. On the table is a lamp, and a few magazines. Up Left, a door to the dining room of the asylum. Further to the front a library table, with books, magazines, etc. On the Right of the desk is a French door entering the office of the Superintendent. *Across the Right wall a large couch, back of which a globe stands. Nearer the audience, on the Right, is a bookcase, on which there is a sewing-basket. In front of this a lamp and another comfortable chair. The entire atmosphere is generally an office, yet a sitting room for the* Patients.

(As the Curtain rises Nurse Smith *is at the desk, busily engaged in writing a weekly report. The* Art Teacher *is writing on the window shade, at the Left of the desk. After a few finishing touches she comes forward and we see that she has been drawing a cat. Looking at the audience, and addressing them as if they were her pupils,* Art *speaks:)*

Art. *(Kindly)* What is this, children?

Smith. *(Looking up)* Miss Art, how many times have I told you not to draw on that window-shade?

Art. *(With great dignity)* Silence in the classroom! (Art *walks forward and stands again before her pupils. Meanwhile,* Smith *has erased the cat from the blind and is busy at her report again.)* Children! Notice the detail in this drawing. Notice the aristocratic ears! *(She turns around to point out these things and sees that the cat is erased)* Oh! The cat jumped over the moon, and is gone!

Smith. And you are not to draw on that shade again, Miss Art!

Art. *(With dignity)* Will you kindly let me conduct my class as *I* see fit?

Smith. *(Reasoning with her)* But it's time for your children to have recess.

Art. Oh, well, in that case the class is dismissed. *(Walks across the front of the stage)* Look at those dear children leave their classroom—— Johnny! Stop pulling Gertrude's hair! Sweet children, they'll all be great artists some day, under my artistic hand. *(She skips about the stage)* Oh, joy is me! Joy is me!

Smith. You've had a hard day in the classroom. Why not rest a bit? You must be just worn right out.

Art. *(With a sigh)* No rest for us teachers. No rest for the art teacher. *(As* Art *talks we hear* Music *singing in the hall off* L. *She is very loud and boisterous. She sings the "Anvil Chorus.")* There's that noisy music teacher. Why doesn't she stay in her room, and leave me to my art?

Smith. Now, please be calm, Miss Art. I'm sure that she won't annoy you.

(Music *backs in, as she marches, apparently leading a class in the song. She smiles as she fin-*

ishes. Her back is still to ART *and* SMITH, *who has risen.)*

MUSIC. Children, children! How many times have I told you to give me *all* your power when you sing? *(She sings boisterously)* "And peace and union, and peace and union, forever more!" *(Speaking again)* Remember now: *"Peace* and *Union!"* *(She skips about the stage.* ART *has endured this interruption as long as she could. She begins going around the stage too, in competition with* MUSIC, *each trying to drown out the noise of the other.* SMITH *tries vainly to stop them.)*
ART. *(As she goes around)* Green, children! What is the color harmony of green? *(Finally* MUSIC *and* ART, *in their skipping around, collide together with a great thud.)*
MUSIC. Get out of my way!
ART. You go back to your room, or—or—I'll paint a picture of you standing on your head, and I'll hang it in the hall for everyone to see.
SMITH. *(Finally getting a word in)* You two mustn't fight. Remember, you are all of the same school and you must maintain co-operation.
ART. But she's disturbing me!
MUSIC. She's always disturbing me.
SMITH. *(A little angry)* Now sit down. *(They do so, rather reluctantly, and poutish.)* Now, remember not to excite yourselves. Just be calm, be quiet and everything will be all right.

(SMITH *goes back to her desk.* MUSIC *sits* L. *and* ART R. *side of the stage, near the audience, and glare at each other. Occasionally one makes a face at the other. Here and all through the play* MUSIC *hums or sings lightly to herself, and* ART, *taking the scissors from the sewing-basket, proceeds to cut out animals and birds from a maga-*

zine's pages. After a moment NURSE JONES *enters* L. *She is a different type than* SMITH, *being generally officious and impatient with these women.)*

JONES. *(Coming up to desk) Oh!* I've just had such a time with that gymnasium teacher. She got violent again and imagined she was teaching her gym class.

SMITH. And when she gets violent it's real.

JONES. Indeed! Do you know that she picked up patient English and threw her almost across the room?

SMITH. *(Laughing)* What was she trying to do? Teach her a new exercise?

JONES. *(Angry)* It may be funny to you, Miss Smith, but in all the years I've spent in this asylum for crazy teachers I've never seen such a panic. It was terrible.

SMITH. Oh, I know. But really they are funny sometimes. You know, it seems that those who came here from the ————— School are always causing trouble.

JONES. You're right. Those who went crazy teaching the pupils there are the worst ever.

HISTORY. *(Enters* L. *at this moment, screaming to the top of her voice. She is in mortal terror of losing her life, it seems)* Don't let them send me to the guillotine! Louie! Louie! Save your Marie Antoinette! Don't let those awful peasants send me to the guillotine! *(She rushes in, falls on her knees and pleads.* JONES *rushes over and gets* HISTORY *to her feet.)*

JONES. Stop this at once! You've got to rest. *(She starts dragging* HISTORY *upstage.)*

HISTORY. They've got me! They're revolting! They'll have my head cut off! Have mercy on Marie Antoinette! Have mercy! *(As they go out* L.

Music *starts singing again, making a tune as she sings, "They've got her! They've got her!"* Art *babbles along with her.)*

Principal. *(Entering* L. *with dignity)* Teachers, what is this wild and unnecessary chatter and noise that I hear? It is echoing and re-echoing into every nook and corner of this building. I, as principal, must ask you teachers to stop this unseemly noise before it becomes necessary for me to use drastic measures. I feel that—— *(The other* Teachers *have stopped the noise.* Smith *comes forward.)*

Smith. Now, there, be quiet! You mustn't get so excited!

Principal. Who's principal of this school? You or me?

Smith. You're the principal, but I'm——

Principal. *(Interrupting)* If I'm the principal, then you must let me conduct my school as I think best.

Smith. *(Trying to reason with her)* But you see, I'm in charge here.

Principal. *(Stopped in her tracks)* She says she's in charge! She's crazy! She's crazy! *(Screaming this, she rushes off* L. *again.* Smith *returns to her seat and* Art *and* Music *begin their noise again.* Mr. Arthur, *the Superintendent, comes from his office,* R.C.*)*

Arthur. Here, here! What is this noise? Can't you keep these patients quiet, Miss Smith?

Smith. But I don't know what to do about them. They're almost unmanageable and Miss Jones just told me that she had been having a lot of trouble with some of the others.

Arthur. Well, something will have to be done. *(To* Art *and* Music*)* Now, you two come along with me upstairs. The children are waiting for their teachers. (Mr. Arthur *takes these* Two *out*

L. Smith *sighs and goes back to her desk.* Dr. Van *enters from* R.C.)

Van. Whew! What a day!

Smith. Have you been having your troubles too, Doctor?

Van. Trouble! Say, you don't know the meaning of the word until you've been through what I have today.

Smith. Why, whatever is the matter?

Van. Oh, that insane Doctor from the men's ward escaped again and came over here to see Miss Gym.

Smith. What seems to be the attraction there? They are always escaping from their own buildings and making calls on each other.

Van. Years ago, before they went insane, they were in love, and engaged to be married. Even though they are both crazy now, they still seem to remember that.

Smith. How very sad. I'd never heard that before.

Van. Well, it might be sad if they realized it, but they are perfectly contented with things as they are—only, of course, they would like to be together more.

Smith. You know, I was thinking today that if some outsider came in here they would have a hard time distinguishing between the sane and insane people here.

Van. That's about right. Still, we have to humor them and agree with them in their whims or we'd have more trouble than ever.

Smith. I suppose you wanted to see Mr. Arthur, didn't you, Doctor?

Van. Yes, but there's no hurry.

Smith. I think he'll be back in a moment. He has taken two of the patients to their rooms, to try and quiet them. He is so conscientious.

VAN. Yes. A very fine man, and a fine head for a place like this. Most anyone else would be crazy like the others inside of a week.

SMITH. That's about right.

VAN. I've got something to talk over with him now. It's rather foolish—not particularly good practice for a doctor, but medicines, and straight-jackets, and such things don't seem to help, and so yesterday, when I came upon this thing, quite by accident, I decided it was more help than all the doctors with their medicine.

SMITH. Why, what is it, Doctor?

VAN. I'll tell you, but don't laugh. You know the bell on the front door is the same sort of bell that these teachers have been used to hearing for years and years while they were teaching. So—when they hear the bell, they all stop whatever they are doing and begin to teach.

SMITH. Habits of a lifetime are not easily changed, eh, Doctor?

VAN. That's just it. They are so in the habit of responding to that bell that, however violent or unmanageable they become, they can always be made to come to order with this bell.

SMITH. Splendid, Doctor. Mr. Arthur will be so pleased.

VAN. Well, it's no credit to me. Imagine a doctor resorting to something like that. It's rather like admitting defeat.

ENGLISH. *(During this speech* ENGLISH *has entered* L. *She has a heavy frown on her face and begins screeching)* Ain't, not, isn't! Ain't, not, isn't!

VAN. *(Suddenly)* I'll ring the bell now, and show you the effect. *(Goes out* R.C. *Meanwhile:)*

ENGLISH. He don't: not he doesn't. Ain't, not, isn't! *(The BELL rings.* ENGLISH *straightens up. Very quietly and dignified, she speaks)* Good morning, children. Ain't cha lookin' nice today! You sure does. (SMITH *laughs*. DR. VAN *re-enters* R.C. ENGLISH *sits down at library table* L. *and conducts class.)*

VAN. Well, how was it?

SMITH. It was too funny, Doctor. She was just screaming at her imaginary pupils, and when the bell rang she quietly called her class to order.

VAN. That's great!

ARTHUR. *(Re-enters* L.*)* Hello, there, Doctor!

VAN. Oh, Mr. Arthur, I have been waiting for you. I'd like to see what can be done about that insane doctor from the other ward.

ARTHUR. Oh, dear! Is he on the loose again?

VAN. "Loose" is right! He's so loose he's about to fall apart. He's broken away from his room three times in the last week.

SMITH. And he always comes here to see Miss Gymnasium, and then the trouble begins.

ARTHUR. Well, about all we can do is watch him more closely.

VAN. What a large order that is!

ARTHUR. Well, don't worry about it, Doctor. You're too serious over your work. I was just telling my niece in my letter to her today that I don't know what I'd do without you, but at the same time I don't want you to wear yourself out.

VAN. Well, that's what I'm paid for, Mr. Arthur.

ARTHUR. Forget it. My niece will be here in about two weeks. When she comes I want you to take more time for yourself, and show her a good time too.

VAN. I'd be glad to.

ARTHUR. And now—shall we have a look at the third floor, where I plan to build a sun porch?

VAN. Fine.

ARTHUR. Oh, Miss Smith, will you come along too?

SMITH. *(Rising)* Certainly.

ARTHUR. *(As they exit* R.C.*)* I want you to have a look in on Ward "C."

(ARTHUR, DR. VAN *and* SMITH *exit* R.C. ENGLISH, *who has been sitting quietly during this time, now looks up, and seeing herself alone, gets up and with tremendous strides she goes across the stage, looks in the hall* R.C., *then through the window; to the* L. *door, and then finding that she is alone, begins to take papers from the drawer of the desk. She tears them up, laughing gleefully. After looking about again she takes out more, tears them, and flings them, talking rapidly all the while.)*

ENGLISH. Ain't, not, isn't! D'ye hear! Ain't, *not,* isn't! Don't, not, doesn't! *(She tears more papers. The BELL rings.* ENGLISH *smiles; sits at desk)* Good morning, children. The class will come to order. Sit youse down. What's doin' this mornin'? Shut up! Sit youse down!

(The BELL rings again. NURSE JONES *comes in from* L. *and starts out door* R.C. *to answer. Seeing* ENGLISH, *she stops and speaks to her.)*

JONES. Get away from that desk! *(*JONES *stoops to pick up some of the papers which are most noticeable and* ENGLISH *throws a book at her, snickeringly)* You bad, bad girl! Sit over there. *(She points to chair at* R. ENGLISH *goes to it.* JONES *starts out* R.C. *again. The BELL rings a third time. She exits, to return again in a moment with* MISS WARE, *who is the* SUPERINTENDENT'S *niece. Meanwhile, in the short time that she is alone* ENGLISH *starts over to the desk again, but just gets there as* JONES *returns. She immediately rushes back to the* *chair, and is rocking innocently as they return.* JONES *is speaking to* WARE*)* I'm sorry to have been so long answering the bell, but we were having a little difficulty here.

WARE. That is perfectly all right. I'm Mr. Arthur's niece. Would you mind telling him I am here?

JONES. His niece, eh? I thought you were a new patient. We were expecting one.

WARE. Really?

JONES. Well, most patients look as sane as you do. It's hard to tell, you know.

WARE. I hardly expected such a welcome.

JONES. *(Who has no sense of humor)* Look at her. Doesn't she look sane? (ENGLISH, *during this time, has been making ridiculous faces, but when* JONES *says this she manages to straighten up and look fairly intelligent.* WARE *regards her.)*

WARE. Yes. Isn't she?

JONES. Humph! Crazy as the rest of them. She was an English teacher. Now that she has lost her mind she uses the worst possible English, just to get even for having to be so careful with her grammar during all the years she was teaching.

WARE. How funny!

JONES. You may think it's funny. I think it's sad.

WARE. I didn't mean "laughable"—I merely meant, how peculiar that she should delight in using incorrect English.

JONES. 'Tis peculiar—very.

WARE. *(Slightly "burned up")* Would you please tell my uncle that I'm here?

JONES. Yes, I'll tell him. You stay here, and no one will annoy you. If anyone comes in, just humor them, agree with them. They're perfectly harmless. *(To* ENGLISH*)* This is a new pupil. Teach her something while I'm gone. *(To* MISS WARE*)* Don't be afraid. *(*JONES *exits* R.C.*)*

ENGLISH. *(Studying* WARE*)* Tell me, what youse would t'ink was a definition of a dangling participle? *(Pause)* Tell me quick, see!

WARE. A dangling participle? Let me see——

ENGLISH. *(Going toward desk)* Ah, so you don't know, eh? *(She tears some more papers on the desk)* I'll learn yuh not to know, see? *(She sits down)* Well?

WARE. *(Amused)* Ask me another question.

ENGLISH. Ask you nothin'! Say, do you know enough to say "ain't"?

WARE. Of course.

ENGLISH. Oh, you do, eh? Well, say "ain't."

WARE. *(In a wee, small voice)* "Ain't."

ENGLISH. All right. Now, no more noise in this here dumb class, get me? *(She busies herself at the desk.* WARE *smiles and sits on couch* R. JONES *returns.)*

JONES. Your uncle wasn't expecting you, was he?

WARE. No, not for about two weeks.

JONES. He looked surprised when I told him you were here. But he'll be down in just a moment. *(To* ENGLISH*)* Come here, Miss English. The class in punctuation is upstairs waiting for you.

ENGLISH. *(Coming over to her)* Yeh! Dat's right. De class in puncheration. *(*JONES *and* ENGLISH *exit* L. WARE *looks around. There is a great NOISE off stage and* DR. VAN *enters* R.C. *with* HISTORY.*)*

HISTORY. *(As they come in)* And I taught them about Napoleon, and Washington, and Amos and Andy, and Cleopatra—ah! Now I *am* Cleopatra! *(To* DR. VAN*)* And you are Marc Anthony! What ho, Marc! *(*DR. VAN *has to humor her.* WARE *looks on.)*

VAN. Hi, there, Cleopatra.

History. I'm mad about you, Anthony, mad, do you hear? I'm crazy about you, crazy!

Van. Don't I know it, Cleo!

History. *(Seeing* Ware*)* Look at her! Are you crazy about her, or are you still *mine?* Answer me, Marc!

Van. I lovest only you, my Cleo.

History. *(Walking over to* Ware*)* Who might you be?

Ware. *(Amused)* Well, I might be—the Queen of Sheba.

History. What! My age-old rival hast returned.

Van. *(To* Ware*)* So you're another recruit for this asylum.

Ware. Yes, Marc.

Van. But—I'm not crazy.

Ware. Nooooo, Marc.

History. Come, Marc. Be my Marc. **Leave the** Queen of Sheba or I willest go crazy.

Ware. *(Enjoying herself)* Stay with me, Marc.

History. But, Marc, I willest killest myself. If you don'test sayest you arest mine alone, I'll lettest the poisonous snake takest a bite of my poor flesh. I lovest thou, Marc.

Van. But the Queen of Sheba loves me too. Don't you, Sheba? *(*Ware *nods, smilingly.)* What must I do? What *can* I do? *(Looks from one to the other, then half to himself)* Humor you both, for one thing. *(Then to them* Both, *very dramatically)* Oh, Cleo, Cleo, you poor soul, and Sheba, Sheba, you poor creature. Alas, we shall have to do as Solomon did with the babe. I shall divide my body in two parts and give you each half.

Ware. Oh, no, not that, Doctor!

Van. Ah! That proves it! She would give all of me up rather than harm me. Her love must be the true one, Cleo.

History. My love is as true as the morning sun! Hers is the false!

Ware. Nay, nay!

History. Doest I not knowest?

Van. Oh, woe is me! Woe is me!

History. O. Sheba! You can take him, take him! Leave me to die of the pains of losing him!

Van. *(To* Ware*)* You're new here, aren't you?

Ware. Aye, Marc Anthony, I am new.

Van. Poor Sheba. Crazy as the rest.

Ware. *(Astounded)* But I'm not crazy.

Van. No! Nobody here is.

History. *(With great grief)* Marc, shall I die? (History *is on her knees.* Dr. Van *raises her to her feet.)*

Van. Nay, nay, Cleopatra. I shall devote my time to you, only you. I shall have no more of the Queen of Sheba.

History. Hear what he says, miserable queen. Me, only me, he loves.

Ware. *(Dramatically)* Sad is my heart.

Van. Come, Cleopatra, let us upstairs fly, that we might carry our love to higher places. *(To* Ware*)* Farewell, Sheba. See you around.

Ware. Of course.

History. Art thou coming, Marc?

Van. Great big stairs we'll climb.

History. To feast in love sublime! (Dr. Van *and* History *exit* L. Ware *laughs as they leave. Then she sighs.* Smith *enters* R.C.*)*

Smith. Miss Ware?

Ware. Yes.

Smith. Mr. Arthur will be down in just a moment.

Ware. Thank you.

Smith. He was sorry to be so long, but there is so much to do here always.

Ware. I should think so. I have just been humoring two of the patients myself, and if they are all like that you can deliver me from all such work.

SMITH. Did they annoy you?

WARE. Not at all. But I felt so sorry for them, especially the man. He seemed almost sane at times. He thought I was insane too just because I humored him as the other nurse told me to do.

SMITH. If it was a man, it must have been that insane doctor from the men's ward. His name is J. Manchester-Sullivan. And woe to anyone who doesn't call him by his full name.

WARE. I didn't call him that. The teacher he was with seemed to think he was Marc Anthony and he quite agreed, so that is what I called him.

SMITH. It is a good thing Miss Gym didn't see them. She is very jealous of her Doctor Sullivan.

WARE. Isn't it dangerous for them to be loose like that?

SMITH. No. None of them are vicious. Of course, the doctor shouldn't be here, but if they've gone upstairs they'll catch him. Miss Jones and your uncle are both up there. *(Sits at desk.)*

ARTHUR. *(Comes in* R.C.*)* Florence! My little niece, how are you, dear? *(They embrace.)*

WARE. Oh, Uncle, it's nice to see you.

ARTHUR. And you're all grown up, aren't you?

WARE. Well, of course. You didn't think I'd stay small forever, did you?

ARTHUR. Hm. I'm afraid I did. Well, come over here, girl. Let's have a good old chat. *(He and* WARE *sit on couch.)*

WARE. My head is whirling. I've seen so much in five minutes that I'm worn out.

ARTHUR. Some of the inmates, I suppose?

WARE. Yes. Two of the funniest people. One woman thought she was Cleopatra and the man with her was sure he was Marc Anthony. It was too funny!

ARTHUR. So the insane doctor is loose again. Dear old J. Manchester-Sullivan. It's a wonder he didn't start trying to operate on you. That's his particular delusion.

WARE. Yes, the nurse was telling me about him.

ARTHUR. But let's talk about you. Why are you here so soon? I didn't expect you for two weeks yet.

WARE. Well, as soon as school was finished I thought I'd come right on down here instead of spending the two weeks in town. It was so hot—and then, too, I wanted to find out why you so mysteriously asked me to spend a month here.

ARTHUR. I thought that had something to do with it. Curiosity killed the cat, you know.

WARE. Now tell me, Uncle, what's the secret?

ARTHUR. You're still thinking of becoming a teacher, aren't you?

WARE. Certainly I am. Why?

ARTHUR. Well, I wanted you to come here so you could see what happens to most school-teachers after they've taught about ten years.

WARE. You mean all your patients were school-teachers?

ARTHUR. Exactly. Most of them we have now were teachers in the —————— School, and the men, too, were professors or doctors on the Board, or something connected with education.

WARE. How sad!

ARTHUR. And so I thought you might change your mind—when you saw them all—about becoming a teacher.

WARE. Well, you may as well give up that idea. I can hardly wait until I get through Normal School so that I may start. I love it, and one couldn't go crazy if she loves her work.

ARTHUR. That's what they all say, Florence. But

they eventually go insane—unless they were that way at the start.

WARE. Well—I'll stay a year, if you want me to, but you can't change my mind. *(Rises.)*

ARTHUR. We'll see. We'll see. *(Crosses to* SMITH *at desk)* Oh, Miss Smith, will you please take my niece's suitcase to the guest cottage?

SMITH. *(Rising)* Certainly. (SMITH *takes the suitcase and exits* R.C. ARTHUR *sits on corner of desk.* WARE, *a little peeved, stands away frcm him.* ARTHUR *changes his manner.)*

ARTHUR. Now, Florence, tell me scmething about yourself. Are—are you in love?

FLORENCE. No.

ARTHUR. Now! Don't kid your uncle.

WARE. Really, Uncle, I'm not. You see, I have been studying so much in order to start teaching next term that I haven't had time for boy friends.

ARTHUR. Well, there's no one here you might be interested in—except the doctor. Say! There's an idea. Doctor Van is my assistant and a very fine fellow.

WARE. *(Smiling)* Matchmaker!

ARTHUR. Not at all, but I don't know what I would have done here without him. I hope you'll at least bc nice to him.

WARE. Any person who helps you is always a friend of mine.

ARTHUR. You're a sweet child. You can't be a teacher.

WARE. Well, we'll see.

ARTHUR. *(Looking at watch)* I thought it was about time to eat. I can always tell. *(He feels his stomach)* The teachers can't seem to realize that they're not still in school at their cafeteria. But we're not here to correct them—only to make them as happy and comfortable as possible.

WARE. I'm going to love this.

ARTHUR. Remember not to laugh at them, though. You'll find it hard sometimes, but always try to be serious and do whatever they ask you to do.

WARE. *(Laughing)* Well, as long as it's within the bounds of reason.

SMITH. *(Re-entering* R.C.*)* The guest cottage is ready now, Mr. Arthur.

ARTHUR. Fine. And now, will you announce lunch?

SMITH. Yes, surely. (SMITH *goes out* R.C.*)*

WARE. Say, where is this Doctor Van that I am to meet?

ARTHUR. He'll be in for lunch. He's probably been busy all morning. He always is.

WARE. And will I be able to talk to the nurses, and ask them questions? *(There is a great RACKET outside* R.C. *as the* NURSES *start down the stairs with the* TEACHERS.*)*

ARTHUR. You are to make yourself completely at home.

WARE. Ho! You talk as if I were a patient.

(The door opens and the TEACHERS *enter from* R.C. SMITH *leads, then the* TEACHERS *and then* JONES.*)*

PRINCIPAL. *(As they come in)* I am the Principal, as you all know, and I am about to call a meeting. *(The* TEACHERS, *now in a line across the stage, with* SMITH *and* JONES *at either end, all scream.)* Before you dismiss your classes for lunch, I must insist that two of you take yard duty, two will be appointed for hall duty, and two for lunch duty, and——

ENGLISH. *(Interrupting)* I ain't a gonna!

MUSIC. *(Singing)* Neither am I! Neither am I!

History. Thou must not countest on me.

Principal. Silence! I am the Principal!

All. *(Singing)* She is the Principal! She is the Principal!

Principal. Yes! I am the Principal!

All. *(Skipping around as they sing)* Yes! She is the Principal! Yes, she is the Principal! (Jones *and* Smith *and* Arthur *try to get them into line again.* Ware *cannot help but laugh at them.)*

Jones. Back in line, teachers! Quiet!

Arthur. Teachers! I don't believe that it will be necessary for anyone to be on duty.

Principal. *(Pushing him back)* I am the Principal! My word is law!

All. *(Singing again, but in their places)* Her word is law! Her word is law!

Principal. Quiet! We will eat lunch in the teachers' room. When I give the signal, march!

(Dr. Van *enters* l., *and goes across to* Arthur.)

Arthur. Florence, I want you to meet——
(WARN *Curtain.)*

(The BELL rings. There is a great bedlam as each Teacher *begins to teach her class. The* Nurses *try to quiet them.)*

Arthur. Answer the door, please, Miss Jones. (Arthur *and* Miss Smith *start the* Teachers *out* l. Jones *exits* r.c. *to answer the door.* Ware *and* Dr. Van *stand together, each thinking the other insane. As* Arthur *gets the* Teachers *out of the room he sees the* Two *together)* Oh, you have met? *(He goes on out* l. *with the* Teachers.)

Ware. Sure, I know you—you're Marc Anthony.

Van. Yes, and you're the Queen of Sheba.

WARE. Yes, Marc.

VAN. May I escort you to the feast?

WARE. Oh, but Cleopatra. Won't she be angry?

VAN. Nay, nay. She shall not know. *(Arm in arm, they exit* L. *as—)*

THE CURTAIN FALLS

ACT TWO

*(As the Curtain rises, S*MITH *is at the desk. Seated around the stage are all the insane T*EACHERS. A*LL are talking, each trying to outdo the others. It is just a general ad lib. which is played until the laughs stop. Then J*ONES *comes from* R.C.*)*

JONES. *(At door)* Will you come in, please, Miss Smith? Mr. Arthur would like to see you.
SMITH. Certainly, I'll be right in.
JONES. *(Halfway in)* And Miss Smith——
SMITH. Yes?
JONES. Have you the report ready for today?
SMITH. *(Holding up report)* It will be ready in about ten minutes. I've been at it nearly two hours now.
JONES. I know. I used to make it out. *(Exits* R.C.*)*
SMITH. *(To* TEACHERS*)* Now I hope you will conduct your classes quietly while I am out.
ALL. *(Ad lib.)* Of course, yes, sure, certainly, yeah! *(Etc., etc.)*
SMITH. That's nice. Now I'll be right back.

(As S*MITH exits* R.C.*,* P*RINCIPAL rushes to the desk from* L. *and* M*USIC from* R. P*RINCIPAL gets there frst and immediately begins to conduct a teacher's meeting. At first each* TE*ACHER furtively looks toward the* R C. *door as if they fear that* M*R.* ARTHUR *will come out and spoil their fun. But gradually each one raises her voice*

above the other until PRINCIPAL *raps on the desk. For a moment they are quiet, thinking of the old days when they really did obey her.)*

PRINCIPAL. Now in today's teacher's meeting we will——

MUSIC. *(Interrupting)* We will sing on page one hundred and eighty-four.

ART. *(Interrupting)* The round circular movement is more graceful, but new modern Art—— *(She draws on the window shade as she talks)* —is stressing the straight line.

PRINCIPAL. Order, please, ladies.

ENGLISH. *(Interrupting)* Ain't you kids goin' to keep quiet? *(Again they* ALL *begin to talk at once.* HISTORY *commands their attention again for the moment.)*

HISTORY. I must have it quiet at once. *(They* ALL *listen to what she is going to say.* HISTORY *walks up front and begins to teach)* Hannibal crossed the Delaware in the year fourteen ninety-two. That was during the war of eighteen twelve. Now who can tell me just what was the condition of Armenia at that time?

ART. *(Cutting in. She picks up the report that* SMITH *has been working on and cuts into it as she talks)* Now—so much for our drawing. People— have you all brought your scissors today? All raise your hands who didn't forget your scissors. Fine! Now, holding the paper like this——

PRINCIPAL. *(As each of these* TEACHERS *cut in on the dialogue of the other there is not a sudden stop, but rather one seems to drown out the other)* On the question of yard duty. I find that so many of you teachers are using the swings and athletic bars and other playground vehicles that the children have no place to play. After due consideration, in order to eliminate trouble along these lines, we shall limit hours as follows: Children will have the playground from nine until three o'clock and the teachers from three o'clock on. To do this, we will have to dismiss all classes which occur between nine and three. School will dismiss at three-fifteen, as usual.

ART. *(Again being heard)* Now hold the paper like this—now cut in just a little way—not too far, now. *(She cuts the paper in two. Noticing this, she shrugs her shoulders and begins again on one of the halves)* Now, curving upwards, slightly as you go —there now—open the paper. *(She does so, with no design resulting.)*

GYM. *(Cutting in. She stands up. During all the previous dialogue, to which she has been oblivious, she has been rocking in chair R., with arms in, against chest and then way out to the sides. Now, as she gets the floor, she does a series of vigorous exercises as she talks)* These bodily contortions increase the mileage per gallon. I have known old dilapidated bodies to be completely revitalized in a few short years by this remarkable exercise. Now, putting the left hand on the right ear thus—— *(She demonstrates)* —and maneuvering the left leg thus—— Now say, "Aaaaaaaahhhh——"

ART. *(Interrupting)* Now you see? That's what I say, class. You never pay attention, and this sort of thing is the result. Had you followed me more closely—— Oh, I don't know what I am going to do with you. This just shows you weren't listening. *(She holds up the paper)* Look at that, you—you—

MUSIC. *(Coming into the limelight)* Now we will begin again—no more interruptions, please. We will sing "Old Black Joe."

(As MUSIC *begins to sing, the rest of the group who have been quiet as long as it is physically possible for them,* ALL *begin to talk again.)*   *(Together)*

PRINCIPAL. As to the subject of attendance, while we all know so well that illness among our youngsters cannot be helped, still we must admit that all children use every possible excuse to remain home from school. I find in looking over our records from last year that attendance was then two and one-half percent higher than at the present time. Something must be done about it. Have you any suggestions? *(Etc., etc.)*

HISTORY. *(At the same time)* Armenia, as Willie said—you have your lesson very well today, Willie—Armenia was a war-torn nation at that time. What with the Chilean army on the right—or was it left?—no, the right, and the army of two hundred strong belonging to Lord Zilch. And the troops of Amenhotep on the left, besieging the entire Southern front— *(Etc., etc., etc.)*

GYM. *(Simultaneously)* Another exercise to increase the mental and thought perceptiveness is the well-known Yogi, taught us first by the natives in the wilds of western Iowa. *(She does some ridiculous exercise)* Eating properly and sleeping a little is also conducive to gout, headaches, and good health in general. Yeast is a good thing to stimulate the flow of the red corpuscles—— *(Etc., etc., etc.)*

(This scene is one general noise and none of the lines are heard individually. After about a moment of this,

} *(Together)*

in which time it has arisen to a bed-
lam, Mr. Arthur, Smith *and*
Jones *come in from* r.c., *unable to*
endure the noise any longer. At
first the Teachers *do not see them,*
but when Arthur *raps for order* *(Together)*
they immediately become quiet, and
take seats again. Principal *stays*
at the desk and Music *sits on the*
long couch. Others *remain in their*
former positions.)

Arthur. *(As they enter)* Ladies! Ladies! School is out. The pupils have gone! You are only wearing yourselves out so that you won't be able to teach tomorrow.

English. Ain't gonna teach tomorry? Whad'ya mean? I'm here every day, ain't I?

Smith. *(Taking her arm)* Indeed you are, Miss English. And maybe you don't think the Board appreciates it.

Jones. *(To the* Others*)* Now let's go upstairs and rest. How's that?

English. That ain't so hot. I ain't tired a bit.

History. I am. I'll go along with you. *(She smiles knowingly and wisely at* Music, *who is just behind her. She winks, and taps her head. She is just humoring the "insane"* Nurse.*)*

Jones. *(Taking* History *and* Music *off* L.*)* Let's go on up, shall we?

Music. *(Re-entering)* Just one moment—until I dismiss these children. *(To her imaginary class)* You may all go now, children. Jimmy, you stay tomorrow night, instead of tonight. Teacher is busy now—— *(But before she finishes* Jones *has dragged her off* L. *While* Jones *is busy with* Music, His-tory *sneaks back.)*

History. Mary, don't forget to turn in that tablet tomorrow. You are three days late now with the death of Queen Elizabeth. (JONES, *thoroughly exasperated, yanks her off* L. *rather roughly. Meanwhile* SMITH *sees* ART *at the blind again.*)

SMITH. Aren't you ashamed, Miss Art, writing on that blind again?

ART. But I had to explain the arc. You see—— *(She picks up the shredded report)* They can't seem to get the idea.

SMITH. *(Woefully)* Oh! My report! Oh, Art! What follies are committed in thy name.

ART. You know—I've often though that same thing.

SMITH. *(Taking* ART *and* PRINCIPAL L.*)* Mrs. Principal, can't something be done to abolish Art in the schools?

PRINCIPAL. *(She is going out* L.*)* I'll take it up in the next meeting. I certainly will.

ART. *(Also exiting* L.*)* Oh, you wouldn't do that! Art is Art! For Art's sake——

SMITH. *(Dragging them)* For Heaven's sake, come along. (ART, PRINCIPAL *and* SMITH *exit* L. GYM *has hidden back of the couch,* R., *unnoticed by the* OTHERS.)

ARTHUR. Go ahead, Miss English. Right after them. The meeting will be continued upstairs.

ENGLISH. Oh, yeah? Yuh can't fool me. They're a-gonna put us ta bed! *(She exits* L. *unwillingly.* ARTHUR *sighs in relief.* WARE *enters* R.C.*)*

WARE. What's all the trouble, Uncle?

ARTHUR. Nothing, my dear, nothing. Just a teachers' meeting interrupted.

WARE. It's so difficult to handle them. I should think it would wear you right out.

ARTHUR. Oh, I enjoy it. Only, as I've already told you—I'd hate to see you among them some day.

WARE. *(Laughing)* Don't worry, I——

ARTHUR. So you haven't seen enough yet to make you change your mind about teaching?

WARE. No. I'm still stubborn, if you want to call it that.

ARTHUR. Well, I'll give you a week. And now you'll have to excuse me—I must go over to the other building.

WARE. We haven't had much time together yet.

ARTHUR. I know. But I'll hurry right back.

WARE. I'll be waiting. Hurry! (ARTHUR *has gone out* R.C. WARE *walks out* L. *slowly. After she has gone* GYM *peeks above the couch.*)

GYM. *(Whispering)* Have they gone yet, children? *(She looks around cautiously and then comes from behind the couch)* Good! Now we can continue our exercises. *(As she begins* DOCTOR SULLIVAN *appears at the window. He enjoys the scene immensely.)* Now, with hands high above the head, like this—— *(She demonstrates.* SULLIVAN *comes around to* L. *door and watches.)* Now bend from the waist—— *(She does so, with hands and head down so that she sees between her legs. The first two or three times she doesn't see* SULLIVAN*)* Ready, now—one, two, three, four, one, two, three, four, one—— *(At this point she sees* SULLIVAN, *and when she comes up her expression is very coy, for this is her "boy friend" coming to call again. She continues with the exercise, however, and each time she goes down* SULLIVAN *peeks at her. When she is up he hides behind the door. Thus they play a game of hide and seek.)* —two, three, four, one, two, three, four—— *(Etc., etc.)*

SULLIVAN. *(Finally coming in)* Splendid, my dear. Splendid! Fine work you are doing. *(He is very pompous and exact. He looks out over the audience)* Just look at the healthy bodies on those youngsters. *(Patting her, very patronizingly)* Making strong men and women for the future. I tell you you should be heartily commended for this, heartily!

Gym. *(Coyly)* Oh, Doctor!

Sullivan. But you'll drive me out of business if you're not careful.

Gym. *(Worried)* Oh, Doctor!

Sullivan. *(Looking at the audience)* There's simply no place for a Doctor among such healthy bodies as these.

Gym. *(Happily)* But we'll open a school of gymnastics. I'll teach you calisthenics, and we'll——

Sullivan. *(Not so "hot")* And give up doctoring?

Gym. Yes! *(Visualizing, as if on a sign)* The Gym and Sullivan School of Health!

Sullivan. *(With dignity)* J. Manchester-Sullivan, if you please.

Gym. Your pardon, Doctor. We'll have to have the sign lengthened. But how does it sound?

Sullivan. *(Coming around)* It does read rather well.

Gym. *(Continuing)* Sullivan and Gym, P.D.Q.; B.V.D.; A.B.C.; N.Y.C.——

Sullivan. And D.T.—We'll do it!

Gym. Specializing in Rolling and Tossing!

Sullivan. *(Painting the sign in the air)* Five dollars the course.

Gym. Ten dollars would be better.

Sullivan. Think so?—Hmmm, perhaps. *(He appears to erase the "five" and put up a "ten.")*

Gym. *(Studying the sign)* We'll be rich, Doctor, rich!

Sullivan. Ah, marvelous, splendid!

Gym. *(Embracing him)* Oh, Doc! Why didn't we think of this before?

Sullivan. But—but after all, I have my patients. Who's to take care of them?

Gym. *(Never at loss)* Well, we'll put them

through our School of Health. They'll forget they were ever sick.

SULLIVAN. Capital, splendid, fine! Let's see—for appendicitis: Up at six o'clock, an hour's horseback ride——

GYM. *(Helping. This scene is played very fast)* Back and into a cold shower——

SULLIVAN. Then a big breakfast——

GYM. Oh, we'll have to have a cook.

SULLIVAN. I have it! We'll cure this Doctor that runs around here. He can be our cook!

GYM. Then, after breakfast?

SULLIVAN. Two hours' workout in the gym, then a mile run——

GYM. Back for lunch.

SULLIVAN. Can't you think of anything but food? It's exercise that's going to do the trick. Now if they must eat lunch, we'll rush them through that and then a swim in the adjoining pool. Then—then—just what would you advise next?

GYM. I'm inclined to think that the appendix would be gone by then.

SULLIVAN. Oh, undoubtedly. Still, we'll want to make it last a day at least. No failures, you know.

GYM. Indeed not! But we can plan the rest of that later.

SULLIVAN. Now let's plan the procedure for rheumatism patients.

GYM. Well, I think, to start with a good——

SMITH. *(From off L.)* Miss Gym! Miss Gym! *(Both* GYM *and* SULLIVAN *are startled.)*

GYM. We'll never get our gymnasium planned with those crazy people around. Let's hide! *(*EACH *tries to start out, but gets in the way of the other. Finally* GYM *runs out* R.C. SULLIVAN *goes to door* L., *then to door* R.C., *and then starts out* L., *but hears* NURSES *coming, so dashes behind couch just before* SMITH *and* JONES *enter* L. *They are very excited.)*

SMITH. Miss Gym! Miss Gym! (JONES *goes out* L., *calling all the time.* SMITH *goes to* ARTHUR'S *office* R.C., *then around the room. After a few sec-onds* JONES *returns, followed by* WARE.)

WARE. I've been right in there all the time. I'm sure I'd have seen her——

JONES. Well, we'll have to go out and look for her, that's all.

SMITH. I'll bet she has gone looking for Doctor Sullivan.

JONES. Probably. They can't be kept apart for long.

SMITH. Where is Mr. Arthur, Miss Ware?

WARE. He said he was going to the other build-ing.

JONES. Thank you. Come, we'll go over there. (*They exit quickly,* R.C. WARE *starts back to room* L. SULLIVAN *comes from behind the couch, and speaks to* WARE, *very gracious and dignified.*)

SULLIVAN. How do you do?

WARE. (*Startled*) Oh, who are you?

SULLIVAN. Why, I am the Doctor here. And may I inquire as to your identity?

WARE. Oh, pardon me, Doctor. I'm a bit on edge, I guess. Things are so sudden and surprising here.

SULLIVAN. Yes, I've found that to be very true. But who are you?

WARE. I'm Mr. Arthur's niece. He told me you would be over to meet me soon, but I didn't ex-pect you just at that moment.

SULLIVAN. I'm so happy to know you, Miss. Your uncle is a very fine man.

WARE. Well—he thinks a lot of you too, Doctor.

SULLIVAN. That makes me very happy.

WARE. I hope you aren't neglecting your patients just to come and see me?

SULLIVAN. Indeed not, I never neglect them—in

fact, I have just come upon a plan of curing these poor unfortunates. It will revolutionize the whole insane industry.

WARE. How marvelous, Doctor. What a great boon to humanity!

SULLIVAN. Yes, but I take little credit. The whole thing came to me rather as an accident. I'm being very sane about the whole affair.

WARE. Can you tell me anything about it, or—or is it too much of a secret yet?

SULLIVAN. Not at all—I should say not. You see, the hypochondriacal hypothesis of unconventionalization is extremely xenophobic, and eulenthic.

WARE. *(Incredulous)* Really?

SULLIVAN. Yes, oh, yes. Extremely eulenthic; in fact, I might even go so far as to say syllogistic— I *will* say syllogistic.

WARE. But——

SULLIVAN. *(Interrupting)* Ah, but! That's just it! There's why my new theory is sure to prosper. Instead of the present treatment for this ichthyophagus, or perineurinium, we will use exercise.

WARE. Well, at least I understand that.

SULLIVAN. Now never you mind, child. I'll make it all very clear to you presently.

WARE. I never hope to understand all this—but could you tell me one thing?

SULLIVAN. *(Making a conquest)* Certainly! Certainly! I'll tell you anything!

WARE. Is—is the insane Doctor over in the other building hopeless? Is he beyond cure?

SULLIVAN. *(Exacting)* Well, yes! (WARE's *face drops.)* Ah, and again, no! *(She has hopes again.)* His is that altogether rare combination of icositetrahedron and histriocomorphic insanity.

WARE. Then nothing can be done for him?

SULLIVAN. Up until today—no! But with this new discovery of mine it will be simple, quite simple. Do you know that I intend to release all of the patients tomorrow? *All* of them! And *each* and *every* one will be entirely cured!

WARE. Oh, how happy my uncle will be. It will make this place world renowned.

SULLIVAN. *(Thoughtfully)* I've got to try it on someone, though, first.

WARE. *(Disappointed)* Oh, then you're not sure of it?

SULLIVAN. Why, just as sure as I'm sane. It's that I want someone whom I've cured to take right up and show your uncle. He wouldn't believe it possible otherwise.

WARE. *(Suddenly)* Why not the Doctor? I feel sure that he can be cured.

SULLIVAN. But he is quite dangerous—quite. I couldn't handle him, alone. No, we'd better try someone else.

WARE. But I could help you, Doctor, and the nurses.

SULLIVAN. *(Not convinced)* No, I'm afraid we'll have to leave him. Now, take that woman who wakes me every morning with her singing. She'd be the one to start with. Oh!—what I could do to her!

WARE. For my sake—wouldn't you cure him first? For my sake——? I'd be so grateful to you.

SULLIVAN. *(Relenting a little)* Well, I——

WARE. I knew you would. Now I'll go get him now.

SULLIVAN. No! No! He'd never come willingly. Now sit down a moment—— Let me think.

WARE. But——

SULLIVAN. My better judgment strongly advises me against this, but I'll do it.

WARE. Thank you, Doctor. I knew you would. Thank you so much.

SULLIVAN. Now listen—this will be our plan—

We can't let him know what we are going to do or he would fight against it. Therefore we'll have to take him by surprise. This very night when he comes in——

WARE. But he may not.

SULLIVAN. Never you fear. He always gets in some way, and when he does you keep his attention, and the nurses and I will rush in, and——

WARE. Oh, but you might hurt him!

SULLIVAN. Nonsense! Now let's see—we'll take him in on the table in your uncle's office.

WARE. Why not in the hospital room?

SULLIVAN. *(Never to be downed)* Well—well—we couldn't get him that far. He'll be howling and kicking, and—well, we just couldn't do it.

WARE. And then what next, Doctor?

SULLIVAN. *(A little insane)* Ah, then what? Then what! Then, child, my life's dream will be realized. I've always dreamed, and waited, and yearned for this chance and now it has come to me —and I can thank you for it——

WARE. But I didn't help——

SULLIVAN. Yes, you did, my dear. You've been the inspiration of the whole thing.

WARE. But——

SULLIVAN. Now don't deny it. I always give the credit where it is due. But now we must get back to our plans. *(During the last three or four speeches* GYM *has been watching them through the window. She is insanely jealous.)*

WARE. I'll tell the nurses to be here at—— But supposing he doesn't come here?

SULLIVAN. Now don't worry. It's all going to work out splendidly. Tonight! Tonight—— *(He stands up, throwing his arms in the air exultantly, and as he turns toward the door* L. *he sees* GYM *standing there, threateningly. He runs back to* WARE *and stands behind her, half hiding)* Oh!

GYM. *(Starting into the room from* L.*)* And after all our plans together for a wonderful gymnasium.

WARE. *(Startled)* Oh! Who's that?

SULLIVAN. *(Shivering)* P-pay no attention to her. J-just humor h-her!

WARE. But it's Miss Gym. They are looking all over for her. She should be upstairs in bed. *(As* SULLIVAN *goes to reply,* GYM *starts after* WARE. SULLIVAN *intervenes.)*

GYM. My gymnasium came tumbling down, and the dumb-bells came tumbling after, and you're the cause of it—you!

SULLIVAN. Now, let's handle this sanely, and sensibly, ladies!

GYM. *(Tearfully)* No gymnasium! No gymnasium!

WARE. There, there! I'm sure the Doctor meant nothing at all. We——

SULLIVAN. Absolutely not. Nothing at all. Nothing——

GYM. *(Sobbing)* After that nice sign we painted! Take my name down! Take my name down! *(She points to the imaginary sign.* WARE *stares in amazement.)*

SULLIVAN. But I was only telling her——

GYM. *(Starting after him)* Exercising your charms instead of your body! *(They run around with* WARE *between them as a pivot.)* I'll teach you! I'll teach you to——

WARE. Stop! Please stop! We'll be your pupils, or anything—only please stop!

SULLIVAN. *(Panting as he runs over to table)* Yes, please stop. We meant nothing—honestly!

GYM. *(Around the table after him)* You! You! I'll——

(The door R.C. *opens and* VAN *enters. He stops in amazement.)*

VAN. Here! Here! What is going on here!

GYM. Oh, you don't know. You'd never believe me if I told you. That man—*(Pointing to* SULLIVAN*)* —and that girl—*(To* WARE*)* —are planning to——

SULLIVAN. Stop her—don't let her tell him—— *(He runs around and manages to throw* DR. VAN *to the floor. He sits on him, screaming)* We have him! We have him!

VAN. Stop this at once! What are you doing? Release me! Here!

SULLIVAN. *(Loudly)* Now you hold him while I get the nurses. *(*WARE *sits on him.* SULLIVAN *starts out* L., *but* DR. VAN *almost escapes.)*

WARE. But I can't hold him here alone, Doctor. Get Miss Gym to help.

SULLIVAN. *(Cautiously)* Yes, do come and play. Then I'll explain all this afterwards. You see we are going to do what you and I had planned—you know—our School of Health. He is going to be the first——

GYM. *(Joyously)* Oh, really? *(She comes over)* Then I'm sorry, Doctor—I should have trusted you. *(She sits on* DR. VAN. WARE *holds on to his feet.)*

VAN. Help! Help! Let me up, I say!

SULLIVAN. Now—I'll be right back with the nurses. *(Exits* L.*)*

VAN. *(To* WARE*)* Can't you see what you are going to do? Let me up! That crazy man is going upstairs. Stop him! All those women!

WARE. No, you've got to stay here until he comes back.

VAN. But he won't come back, I tell you!

GYM. *(Bouncing on his stomach)* Oh, this is fun! Lots of fun! Good for you, too. It stimulates the gastric juices.

VAN. Please, Sheba, let me go—I——

GYM. Just relax, please, relax. *(*SULLIVAN *comes*

in L. *silently, followed by all the* TEACHERS *in long flannel nightgowns and caps.)*

WARE. What are you doing? Where are the nurses? (SULLIVAN *is gathering the* TEACHERS *around* DR. VAN.)

VAN. *(Terrified)* Let me up! Oh! All those crazy women—something terrible will happen! All crazy——

SULLIVAN. *(Tapping his head)* Isn't it strange that a crazy person always thinks it is the other fellow who is that way?

WARE. Doctor, why all those women? What is wrong? Where are the nurses?

SULLIVAN. I couldn't find them, but these will do just as well. Why, can't you see? They're perfectly harmless. *(All the* TEACHERS *nod ridiculously and their caps bob up and down.)*

WARE. I know, but if something——

SULLIVAN. *(Impatient)* Now don't worry—it's all working out fine. *(To the* TEACHERS*)* You take this arm. Now you take this one. You his head. *(To* GYM, *who is still sitting on* DR. VAN*)* Get up, Miss Gym!

GYM. Oh, must I? I'm doing him lots of good.

SULLIVAN. *(Beside himself)* I know, I know! But we must get down to business. (GYM *arises reluctantly.* SULLIVAN *goes on)* You take his right leg, and you his left. Fine, now—— (TEACHERS *follow his orders.)*

WARE. *(Interrupting)* Are you sure this is advisable? I hardly thought——

SULLIVAN. In fifteen minutes he'll be as well as you or I—— Now—into the office there. *(He rubs his hands in glee.* WARE *is distrustful.)* My life's dream—— *(They start off* R.C.*)* —my plans, my hopes, all to be realized!

WARE. Be careful of his head. Oh! You'll drop

him! *(The* TEACHERS *disappear into* R.C. GYM *and* WARE *stand at the door with* SULLIVAN.*)*

SULLIVAN. *(To* WARE*)* Now you go and get more bandages and towels, quick!

WARE. There are some in there, Doctor, already.

SULLIVAN. I know, but I want yards of them! Miles of them! *(To* GYM *as* WARE *exits* L.*)* Now, when we get inside, you lean against the door so no one will disturb us. *(They go inside* R.C.*, closing the door. After a moment* ARTHUR, JONES *and* SMITH *enter* L. *They are all excited and fatigued.)*

JONES. I've been over every inch of the garden.

ARTHUR. That mad doctor gone too is what worries me.

SMITH. *(Entering last)* They must be together.

JONES. Well, if they are, that means trouble sure.

ARTHUR. *(Going to* R.C. *door)* Why! There's someone in my office!

SMITH. It may be your niece.

ARTHUR. Florence! Florence! *(He tries the door again. It doesn't give.)* They're holding it closed!

WARE. *(Coming in* L. *with linens)* What is the matter, Uncle?

ARTHUR. Someone is in there.

WARE. Oh, it's all right. It's only the doctor. He is curing one of the patients and we didn't want you to know until it was all done.

ARTHUR. What was all done?

WARE. The cure! Oh, Uncle, you're rich, you're famous, and you owe it all to this doctor.

JONES. What *is* she talking about?

WARE. The doctor is giving the insane one a treatment. He'll cure him. The man will be sane, Uncle, sane. Aren't you happy?

ARTHUR. Extraordinary! Doctor Van would never do such a thing—in my office, too! And that insane teacher with him.

WARE. All of the teachers are with him.

JONES. The girl is crazy too! Oh, I'm so sorry, Mr. Arthur.

VAN. *(Screaming from within)* Stop it! Let me out of here! Help!

ARTHUR. Why, that's Doctor Van! What is going on in there? *(He rattles the R.C. door.)*

VAN. *(Screaming again)* Stop it at once! Oh! Help!

ARTHUR. *(Suddenly)* I know! Florence! You've had those doctors mixed. The sane and the insane. J. Manchester-Sullivan is operating on our doctor with a horde of insane women for assistants.

SMITH. I told you it was hard to tell who is sane here. *(Pause.)* Listen! I have it! The bell! You know, the doorbell! Doctor Van told you how they reacted to it.

ARTHUR. That's right! Ring it quick! *(JONES and SMITH go out L.)*

WARE. *I'm so sorry.* Oh, they mustn't have hurt him! They can't have done anything to——

(The BELL rings. After a second the R.C. door flies open and GYM comes out first, followed by the other TEACHERS. They all bow and say "good morning" to their pupils and take their various places on the stage. ARTHUR rushes into the office. There is a great bedlam. SULLIVAN comes out, moaning.)
                                        (WARN Curtain.)

SULLIVAN. *(Sadly)* What's the matter? Oh! My experiment is ruined! Ruined utterly! I'll never get such a golden opportunity again! Oh!

(The noise continues. ARTHUR comes out, bringing DR. VAN. The latter is swathed in bandages from head to foot and is hanging on ARTHUR for support. SMITH and JONES have returned

before this and are trying to quiet the TEACH-
ERS.)

VAN. *(As he enters* R.C.*)* Oh, get these things
off! Help!
ARTHUR. *(Trying to be heard)* Stop that noise.
(The TEACHERS *calm down somewhat.)* So sorry,
Doctor. It was all a mistake, an error.
VAN. *(Pointing to* WARE*)* Put that girl in a
padded cell. She's not like the rest. She's danger-
ous! Beyond hope!
WARE. *(Incredulous)* Me? Insane?
ARTHUR. A hideous mistake, Doctor. This is
Florence Ware, my niece. Florence, this is Doctor
Van.
WARE. Then—then you're not insane?
VAN. *(Looking around.* GYM *is consoling* SUL-
LIVAN. ART *is drawing on the window shade.* HIS-
TORY *is whirling the globe.* SMITH *and* JONES *are
trying to stop them.* DR. VAN *surveys all this, then)*
Insane? I—I don't know. I once thought I was
all right, but I don't know who's crazy now. *(He
collapses.* EVERYONE *rushes over to him as—)*

THE CURTAIN FALLS

ACT THREE

The next morning.

As the Curtain rises Arthur *is leaning over the body of* Dr. Van *on the couch. After a moment* Smith *enters from* L.

Smith. Is there any change, Mr. Arthur?

Arthur. Not yet. I called in a fine specialist from the outside to see what he could do. He has just left.

Smith. Did he offer much encouragement?

Arthur. It's a bit too soon to tell. The whole thing was a shock, and then, too, his head was injured some way in there.

Smith. How terrible! That insane Sullivan person will have to be chained before he does any more serious damage.

Arthur. Indeed. We have him under observation now, but I'm afraid it's like closing the barn door after the horse is gone. I never dreamed he would ever be dangerous.

Smith. Well—none of them have been up till now.

Arthur. I suppose they had no intention of being really violent.

Smith. But—but what can we do now? This standing around seems so useless.

Arthur. We can do nothing until Doctor Van comes to. (Ware *enters* R.C. *sadly. She is wearing a hat and coat and has a suitcase, the one which she had in the First Act.* SMITH *sits at desk.)* Florence, darling! Where are you going?

WARE. I'm going back, Uncle. It has been great to see you, but I can't look Doctor Van in the face after my ridiculous actions, so——

ARTHUR. But wait, at least, until he comes to.

WARE. Oh, no. I want to get away before he does. Oh! I've been so foolish. I ought to have known that man was crazy—that Sullivan. Now that I think back, I can't imagine how he could have fooled me so.

ARTHUR. It's happened many times before, dear. Many, many times there is just a thin line between sanity and insanity.

WARE. I know, I know. But it doesn't excuse me. Tell him how sorry I am, won't you? Try to make him understand it all.

ARTHUR. Of course he'll understand—but please wait.

WARE. *(Reminiscently)* Did you hear him—just before he fainted? He looked at me and said, "Put that woman in chains—she's not like the rest. She's dangerous."

ARTHUR. That was just because he thought that—

WARE. *(Interrupting)* I know, but he thought pretty nearly right, at that. *(She walks over to the couch)* Oh, just think! It may affect him for life!

VAN. *(As she leans over him, he comes out of it)* Hello, Sheba!

WARE. *(Starting away)* Oh!

VAN. *(Rising)* Sheba! Sheba! Stay here with me. Am I not your Marc Anthony any more?

WARE. *(Sadly)* Oh, don't make fun of me, Doctor. It was such a mistake.

VAN. Our love a mistake? Sheba, why, what is wrong? *(As* WARE *is about to reply,* ARTHUR *comes over to* VAN.)

ARTHUR. Stop! Listen, Florence. Doctor! (DR.

VAN *ignores him.)* Doctor!—Don't you know me?

VAN. Sheba, are you being untrue to me? Who is this man?

ARTHUR. You see, Florence, he doesn't know what he is saying.

SMITH. You mean he's out of his head still.

ARTHUR. Yes. But he'll——

WARE. You're right, Uncle. Oh, how terrible, and all my fault.

ARTHUR. Now, don't take it that way. He'll come around all right. You just be patient and we will do all we can for him.

VAN. Sheba! Come with me and leave yon stranger, else I drive my trusty sword through him —and to the hilt, too! (DR. VAN *starts toward* ARTHUR. SMITH *comes around from her desk excitedly.)*

SMITH. Shall I call the doctor back again—the one who was just here?

ARTHUR. *(Worried)* Yes, please do. Tell him to come over at once.

SMITH. Very well. If you need me, I'll be in here. *(She exits* L.*)*

GYM. *(Enters from* R.C. *noisily)* Where is Doctor Sullivan? J. Manchester-Sullivan! What have you done with him? Doctor! Oh, Doctor!

ARTHUR. Now you must keep quiet, Miss Gym. Something terrible has happened. Please.

GYM. *(To* WARE*)* It's your fault, I know—ever since you came you've caused trouble. It was you who stole my doctor.

WARE. Oh, Uncle, take her away.

GYM. *(Not to be stopped)* Where is he? What have you done with him—and after you both promised me that it wouldn't happen again. Oh!

ARTHUR. Miss Gym, please. Come with me, will you? I'll help you find him?

GYM. *(Seeing* DR. VAN*)* Why, there's our cook! What is he doing here? Doctor Sullivan was going to cure him so he could cook for us in our new gymnasium.

ARTHUR. What? Oh, so you see, Florence, that's what prompted all this. Miss Gym and Doctor Sullivan had planned to try their cure on him anyway. You're not to blame, after all.

VAN. For the last time, Sheba—send these courtiers away that we may be alone—and post sentries at the gates to keep Cleopatra out of here. That woman will not let me rest.

WARE. Uncle—maybe if you all go and leave me to talk to him——

ARTHUR. That might help—if you're not afraid of being alone with him.

WARE. Of course I'm not.

ARTHUR. Then we will come after him as soon as the specialist comes again.

GYM. *(As* ARTHUR *takes her out* L. *she speaks as they go)* There's no use trying to accomplish anything with all these crazy people around. Believe me, it wasn't that way at the ——————— School.

WARE. I was going to leave without seeing you— but I'm so glad I didn't. Now I'm going to help you to get well again.

VAN. *(Dumbly)* Sure, Sheba! You and I are going to get along great. If only we didn't have our subjects to rule. Let's just go away and leave them to care for themselves.

WARE. Doctor Van—don't you remember? You're not crazy. And I'm not either. Didn't Uncle tell you, when they brought you out of there, that I was all right—that it was just a mistake?

VAN. Can't you be carefree and happy as I am? This is love, and springtime. Let's go to my palace. *(Takes her arm)* Come, Sheba, what's the rhyme?

(Thinks it over) "Great big stairs we'll climb——"
Go on. Say it. "To feast in love sublime." *(As
they start out* L. SMITH *enters* L.*)*

WARE. He insists on going out. What can I do?

SMITH. You go right with him. Just keep him
interested until the doctor arrives. We'll send the
doctor right on out to you in the garden.

WARE. *(As they go out)* All right. And please
have him come soon.

VAN. *(As he exits* L.*)* You give me none of
your time, Sheba. Why worry about these subjects?
They can—— *(Etc., etc.* SMITH *takes her desk,
with a sigh.* ARTHUR *enters* L.*)*

ARTHUR. Those teachers upstairs have decided
to have an educational exhibit today.

SMITH. What?!

ARTHUR. Yes, and there's no stopping them.
They seem to think it's the end of the year and
they are all planning now what they are going to do.

SMITH. How do you suppose they ever get all
these ideas?

ARTHUR. There's no telling—but we'd best let
them go. I think they are less trouble when they
are occupied with something.

SMITH. Yes, that's one consolation.

ARTHUR. I think we'll need all our time and attention for Doctor Van. *(NOISE of* TEACHERS
off L.*)* By the way, where is he now?

SMITH. Outside. He insisted that Miss Ware go
with him to his palace. I don't know just where he
thought that was. *(As* TEACHERS *begin to come
in* L.*)*

ARTHUR. *(Going to office)* I'll be in here. I can't
stand that today. *(Exits* R.C.*)*

ART. *(Entering* L.*)* My exhibit will be much
more beautiful with all the whippempoofs my children have drawn.

English. Humph! What's that compared to the essays my kids have writ on puncheration?

Principal. *(Coming in* l. *with notebook)* Then, after the exhibit in the rooms, we will have a teachers' program in the auditorium. I—I am going to sing.

Music. *(Entering* l. *to hear this last)* You're going to sing? Why, you're crazy! I am the music-teacher here. If there must be music, I'll give it, see?

English. There ain't nobody going to sing here. I can't explain these children's work with you howlin'!

Gym. I have it! We'll get up a chorus and all sing.

Music. Fine! And I'll lead. I should lead.

English. Then I'll write the song.

Principal. *I'll* write the song.

English. You ain't a-gonna.

Art. *(Coming in on the argument)* That's not important. Listen: we'll dress up, and I'll design the costumes. *(To* Principal*)* You'll be a whippempoof, the kind my children drew. *(To* Music*)* I can't think of anything mean enough for you. *(To* All*)* What could she be?

English. *(As if that helped!)* I'll dress as a question mark. *(She stands that way.)*

Music. Hah! You won't need to dress any.

English. Is that so? Say, you listen to me. *(She starts after* Music. History *intervenes.)*

History. I've got it! I've got it! We'll give a pageant of History!

Principal. *(Doing the step)* I speak to be Salome!

History. Salome, nothing! Cleopatra is going to be the woman in this show!

Music. I'll be Nero and sing while Rome burns.

ART. *(With her fist shaking)* If you sing, I'll be Rome—and I'll burn right up.

HISTORY. Come, now. Let's have a rehearsal—I'll direct.

PRINCIPAL. I'll direct. I tell you: anything that requires directing, or supervising, or executive ability—I'll do it, see?

ENGLISH. *(After her)* Not while I'm conscious.

ART. *(Picks up a bookend and goes after ENGLISH)* I'll fix that right up!

MUSIC. *(Intervening)* You'll fix nothing. You never could.

HISTORY. *(Angrily)* Please, ladies! *(To PRINCIPAL)* Now, you will be Cæsar.

ART. She will not. She is a whippempoof.

PRINCIPAL. I'm not. I'm Salome.

MUSIC. Oh, dear! What is she?

GYM. I've often wondered.

HISTORY. *(Going right on)* She's Cæsar. I'll be Cleopatra! But who'll be Marc—— *(Remembering)* Where is my Marc?

ENGLISH. *(Guilty-conscience-like)* I ain't got him, honestly. I ain't seen him at all.

PRINCIPAL. I must insist that whoever has her Marc return it right away.

HISTORY. Who's seen my Marc?

ALL. *(Half chanting)* Where is her Marc?

HISTORY. *(Sing-song)* I'll find my Marc!

ALL. *(Same)* We'll find her Marc!

HISTORY. *(Hog-calling)* Oh, Marc!

ALL. *(In full chorus)* Oh, Marc!

MUSIC. *(She steps to the front, blows "C" on her pitch-pipe which she always carries, and, to the tune of "Rigoletto," she sings)*
She wants to know who has her Marc.

ALL. *(Singing "Rigoletto")*
Where's her Marc? Where's her Marc?

HISTORY. *(As* EACH ONE *has her solo line, she steps to the front and adds to the line of* SINGERS*)*
Yes! I want to know who has my Marc.
ALL.
Who has her Marc?
ENGLISH. *(Joining them)*
You ain't got no Marc—he's on a lark.
HISTORY.
I want my Marc.
ART.
Who's got him?
HISTORY.
Marc!
ALL.
Oh, Marc, oh, Marc!
PRINCIPAL. *(Very dramatic)*
We shall find him!
HISTORY.
Yes, we'll find him!
MUSIC. *(Pointing* R.C.*)*
He may be out there!
HISTORY. *(Starting out* R.C.*)*
He may be!
PRINCIPAL. *(Following* MUSIC *and* HISTORY*)*
Oh, he may be!
ALL. *(As they exit* R.C.*)*
He may be there!

(This entire scene is done after the style of grand opera. At the end of this number, all the TEACHERS *have left, leaving only* SMITH, *looking up disgustedly from her work. After a moment* ARTHUR *enters* R.C., *or just at the end of the song.)*

ARTHUR. Is that over with finally?
SMITH. Yes, Mr. Arthur, but they've gone out looking for Doctor Van. Miss History has lost her

Marc. You remember that is what she calls Doctor Van.

Arthur. *(Laughing)* Yes, I know.

Smith. He used to play for hours with her, just to humor her. He was so kind to them all.

Arthur. Yes, that's how Florence got the idea that he was insane.

Smith. You can hardly blame her.

Arthur. *(Nervously)* If that specialist would only arrive.

Smith. I don't believe he has quite had time yet.

Jones. *(Entering* R.C.*)* All these women went out in the garden where Miss Ware was sitting with Doctor Van.

Arthur. Oh, is there anything wrong?

Jones. Well, hardly "wrong"—but they have the Doctor up doing Maypole dances, or something—I couldn't quite follow what it was.

Arthur. You'd better see to them.

Jones. I tell you, there's no handling them. They have an exhibit on their minds and they're absolutely rabid.

Smith. *(Rising)* Maybe between the two of us we'll be able to quiet them somewhat.

Jones. *(As they go out)* We can try. *(*Smith *and* Jones *go out* R.C. *After a moment* Ware *enters* L. *She is downcast.)*

Arthur. Well, I thought you were with the doctor.

Ware. *(Sadly)* I was—but he doesn't need me. He's playing a game of History with those teachers. *(Going to chair at table* L.*)* They insisted on my being the Queen of Sheba, but I couldn't—I just couldn't talk.

Arthur. You're quite worried over Doctor Van, aren't you, dear?

Ware. Surely I am. Aren't you?

Arthur. *(With a smile)* Well, there's no doubt

in my mind but what he will get well again—but it seems to me that you are taking an unusual sort of interest in him.

WARE. *(Rising)* What do you mean, Uncle?— You don't think that I——

ARTHUR. I think just that—that you are falling in love with him.

WARE. *(Flustered)* How absurd. I'm surprised that you would——

ARTHUR. *(Interrupting)* No—it's not absurd. Stranger things have happened.

WARE. But I've only known him one day.

ARTHUR. Yes—but what a day!

WARE. I'll admit that practically everything has happened that could possibly—in that much time. All we need now is a nice healthy cyclone.

JONES. *(Coming in* R.C.*)* The specialist is here. He wants you at once, Mr. Arthur. We have taken Doctor Van to the hospital room.

SMITH. *(Coming in* R.C., *excitedly)* The teachers are looking for Doctor Van. I'm so afraid they will break into the hospital room.

ARTHUR. Bring them in here where you can watch them. Let them do anything just so they won't start wandering around. I'll go to the doctor, at once.

WARE. May I come too, Uncle?

ARTHUR. You'd better not, dear. I'll let you know as soon as anything happens. (ARTHUR *goes out* R.C. WARE *starts out* L. *There is a great NOISE offstage.)*

SMITH. You come with me, Miss Ware. I don't imagine you feel like listening to them.

WARE. *(As she goes out)* I'm afraid I don't.

(The TEACHERS *begin to enter* R.C., *talking and singing to the top of their voices.* WARE *and*

SMITH *go out* L. *hurriedly.* JONES *takes her place at the desk.)*

ALL.
Marc, oh, Marc!
She's lost her Marc!
He's in the park.
Marc, Marc, oh, Marc! *(Etc., etc.)*
JONES. *(Exasperated)* Ladies, please! Can't you go on with the plans for your exhibit? This Marc will return presently.
PRINCIPAL. *(The old sage)* That's a splendid idea! You know there is no use crying over un-crossed bridges after you've eaten them.
ENGLISH. Yes, let's get on with the play.
MUSIC. Where did we leave off? *(She thinks)* Oh, yes, I was singing.
ART. And I was burning up!
HISTORY. *(With a shrug of resignation)* Well, I can't do much without Marc—but—the play *must* go on.
GYM. I think there should be some sort of a dance, don't you?
PRINCIPAL. Oh, we must have a dance.
MUSIC. And a theme song.
GYM. Surely! And then we'll dance to the song.
MUSIC. No, no! The music wouldn't be heard.
ART. *(The old cat)* That's the idea! If we can only make *enough* noise when we dance.
HISTORY. I'll have you know I'm light on my feet!
ENGLISH. But much lighter in yer head!
HISTORY. *(Dramatically)* I'll have you be-headed!
PRINCIPAL. Then I'll be the guillotine! Remember I must be the head man in anything you do.
ENGLISH. But—but don't you think it might hurt?

Music. Not a bit. You'd never realize it.

English. Are yuh shure?

Art. No, you'll never miss your head a bit.

Gym. Won't know it's gone—unless you tell her.

History. Well—let's get down to business. Where shall we build the scaffold?

English. *(Strutting across the stage)* Build it where I'll have ter go upstairs. I wanna make a scrumptious entrance.

Gym. That won't be necessary.

English. Say, who's bein' beheaded here, you or me? Guess I oughta have sumthin' to say!

Gym. *(As she kneels)* Now look. I'll get down like this—and when someone gives the signal——

English. *(Interrupting)* I'll get conked on the burr—is that it?

Principal. *(Coming forward)* Exactly! But— it must be done by a signal from *me!*

History. Fine! And then we can try you for murder, and——

Principal. Murder! I never heard of such a thing.

Music. If you ask me, I think that's the best idea yet.

Principal. *(With dignity)* Ladies! I feel that this rehearsal for an exhibit is fast becoming a festival of felines. (ALL *start around* Principal *in a circle, doing "Meows" and arching their backs like cats.)*

Gym. *(Who is still on her knees)* Say, how long do you think I'm going to play Mother Guillotine?

History. Yes, let's get back to business.

Art. Who was it we were going to behead?

Gym. *(She goes forward on one elbow, like Rodin's "Thinker")* Let me see—— I forget.

English. *(A little timid)* I think it was me, wasn't it?

Principal. Seems like it was, come to think of

it. Still, we ought to be sure. Does anyone remember, definitely?

ENGLISH. I'm quite sure it wuz me, but don't worry, if you find it is a mistake I won't mind a bit. (ENGLISH *puts her head in the arch of* GYM's *back.*)

PRINCIPAL. Be quiet now! You're all peasants who have come into power. When we have this program we will shield the actual sight of the beheading from the audience—like this. (*She stands directly in front of* GYM *and* ENGLISH. HISTORY *observes it all, then:*)

HISTORY. What a shield!

PRINCIPAL. (*To* HISTORY, *angrily*) You stand there! (*To* OTHERS) You there, you there, and you there—no, over here. Fine! Now, when I give the signal——

VAN. (*Entering* R.C. *The* TEACHERS *are all stooped over the* GROUP, *like football players in a huddle*) Well, good day, ladies! Playing football, I see.

HISTORY. (*Coming over to him*) Oh, no, Marc. You are about to witness an execution.

VAN. Is that right? Well, I'm glad I got here in time, but can't we do this outside?

HISTORY. Yes, Marc. If you'll come along too.

VAN. Why, certainly. I'll be right along. Now you go on out there.

HISTORY. Oh, no. Oh, *no!* You've avoided us too many times already. You'll have to come now.

VAN. (*With a sigh*) Oh, all right. (*He heads the line and starts skipping around the room. The* OTHERS *follow him, skipping.* WARE *enters* L., *unnoticed, and stops in amazement. As the* GROUP *reach the door* DR. VAN *steps aside quickly and the* TEACHERS *race out* R.C., *in their speed to get to the execution. When they have all gone out he closes the door quickly.* WARE *walks over to* JONES, *who is still at desk.*)

WARE. Look! There's Doctor Van! What is he doing here?

JONES. *(Rising, as if to go out)* I don't know. I'll call your uncle.

VAN. *(Intervenes)* Stop! I'm all right now. I was only humoring the patients!

WARE. *(Coming forward)* Only "humoring the patients!" I've heard that so much *I'll* go crazy if I hear it again.

VAN. *(With a laugh)* I thought you were that way once.

WARE. That's just it—and I thought you were, too. And when I came in now and saw you skipping about I thought the specialist had been unable to do anything for you.

VAN. Indeed he could. I'm fine now.

JONES. Just what was the trouble, Doctor?

VAN. My head was injured when they took me in there. But the pressure has been released and everything is all right again.

WARE. But doesn't it hurt? Are—are you sure you're all well?

VAN. Well, frankly, it does hurt a little, but I thought I might be needed here—and then I wanted to see you.

WARE. *(Angrily)* Let me tell you something!

VAN. *(Wonderingly)* Yes?

WARE. You'll not see me now, nor ever again, if you don't promise me one thing.

VAN. Why, what's that?

WARE. Promise that you'll give up this—this *humoring the patients!* Think how many things have come about from *humoring the patients!*

VAN. But—but I can't give up my work here.

WARE. You don't have to do that, but you can be a little less one of them, so to speak.

VAN. All right, Florence, I will—on one condition.

WARE. And what's that?

VAN. That you promise me you won't be a teacher. If you'll promise me that, I'll even leave this place. (ARTHUR *and* SMITH *enter* R.C. *to hear* WARE'S *line.)*

WARE. *(After a moment's thought)* All right, I'll do it! I'll give up teaching.

ARTHUR. *(Jubilant)* Aha! I knew you'd do it. That's what I brought her here for, Doctor. I knew when she saw this she'd change her mind. I knew it wouldn't even take a week.

WARE. *(A little coy)* But, Uncle—it wasn't seeing them that did it. (HISTORY *sneaks in,* R.C., *quietly and comes over to* DR. VAN, *taking his arm, and being very bashful.)*

ARTHUR. Then what was it?

WARE. *(Pointing to* DR. VAN*)* It—was—he!

HISTORY. We're waiting for you, Marc. You promised me you'd come along.

ARTHUR. I believe there's going to be a very private conversation here. Come along, Miss History.

HISTORY. But Marc must come too.

ARTHUR. I'm afraid you've lost your Marc, Miss History. But I'll find you another bright, new, shiny one.

HISTORY. *(As she goes out* R.C.*)* Really! Will he be bright, and new, and shiny?

ARTHUR. *(At the* R.C. *door, as an afterthought)* Oh, can't you ladies think of something you should take care of—well, say, in the attic, or the basement, for instance? (SMITH, *who has been talking to* JONES *quietly at the desk since her entrance, smiles knowingly.* JONES *is rather dull.)*

JONES. What do you mean, sir?

SMITH. I think I understand, Mr. Arthur. *(To* JONES, *as she takes her arm)* Come, Miss Jones.

Don't you remember all those places in the basement where we can hide behind the axes?

> *(WARN Curtain.)*

JONES. *(As they go out* L.*)* I don't seem to follow you. *(DR. VAN gives a gesture of despair. It seems as though he is never going to have a moment alone with WARE.)*

SMITH. *(As she exits* L.*, to JONES)* Never mind, I'll draw you a picture. *(She turns to ARTHUR as they exit and gives a knowing sign, like the TEACHERS have used throughout the play to show that someone else is "just a little off." When they have gone DR. VAN gives a sigh of relief.)*

VAN. *(Taking WARE in his arms)* Alone at last!

WARE. Yes, and no more patients to humor. *(Just as they are about to kiss, from every door and window there is a noise, as all of the insane TEACHERS, and even J. MANCHESTER-SULLIVAN, appear. They ALL scream wildly and then, in a chorus:)*

ALL. *Who's Crazy now!*

(DR. VAN and WARE look very embarrassed as they look around. All of the INMATES are shaming them with their fingers as—)

THE CURTAIN FALLS

"WHO'S CRAZY NOW?"

PROPERTY PLOT

ACT I

Papers, writing material, etc. (desk).
Globe (back of couch).
Books, magazines, etc. (library table).
Magazines (small table).
Sewing-basket (bookcase).
Chalk (Art).
Scissors (sewing-basket).
Suitcase (Ware).
Ruler (desk).

ACT II

Flannel nightgown and caps (Teachers).
Bandages and towels (Ware).

ACT III

Suitcase (Ware).
Notebook (Principal).

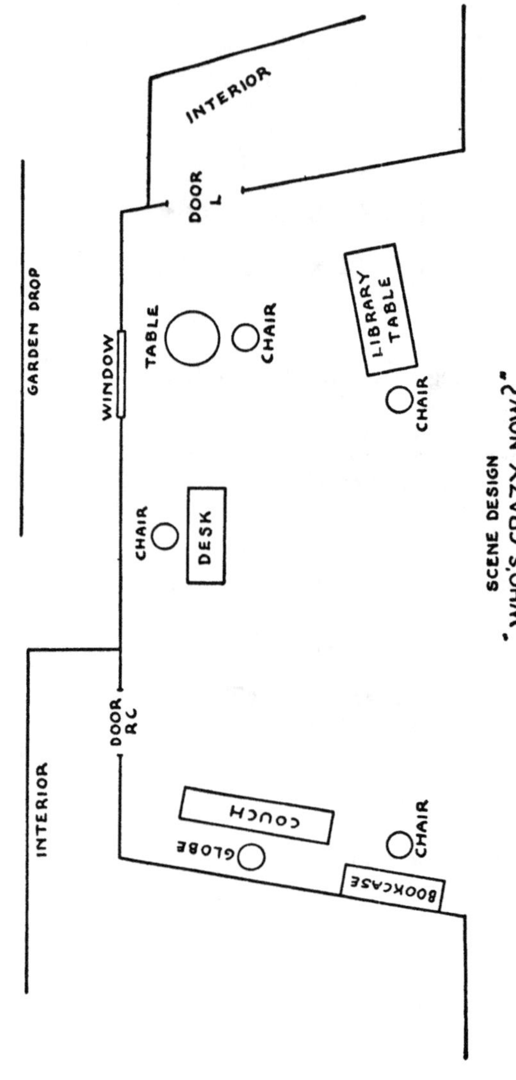

INTERIOR
DOOR L
GARDEN DROP
WINDOW
TABLE
CHAIR
LIBRARY TABLE
CHAIR
DESK
CHAIR
DOOR RC
INTERIOR
COUCH
GLOBE
CHAIR
BOOKCASE
SCENE DESIGN
"WHO'S CRAZY NOW?"

OTHER TITLES AVAILABLE FROM SAMUEL FRENCH

NO SEX PLEASE, WE'RE BRITISH
Anthony Marriott and Alistair Foot

Farce / 7 m, 3 f / Interior

A young bride who lives above a bank with her husband who is the assistant manager, innocently sends a mail order off for some Scandinavian glassware. What comes is Scandinavian pornography. The plot revolves around what is to be done with the veritable floods of pornography, photographs, books, films and eventually girls that threaten to engulf this happy couple. The matter is considerably complicated by the man's mother, his boss, a visiting bank inspector, a police superintendent and a muddled friend who does everything wrong in his reluctant efforts to set everything right, all of which works up to a hilarious ending of closed or slamming doors. This farce ran in London over eight years and also delighted Broadway audiences.

"Titillating and topical."
– NBC TV

"A really funny Broadway show."
– ABC TV